On my beach
there are
many pebbles

by
Leo Lionni

A
MULBERRY
PAPERBACK BOOK
New York

Library of Congress Cataloging in Publication Data
Lionni, Leo, 1910–
On my beach there are many pebbles / Leo Lionni. p. cm.
Summary: Pictures and describes the many different shapes and markings of pebbles—"fishpebbles,"
"peoplepebbles," "letterpebbles"—found on the beach. [1. Pebbles—Fiction.] I. Title. PZ7.L6634On 1995
[E]—dc20 94-6484   CIP AC

First Mulberry Edition, 1995. ISBN 0-688-13284-7
10 9 8 7 6 5 4 3 2 1
Published by arrangement with Astor-Honor Publishing, Inc.

On my beach there are many pebbles

Most are ordinary pebbles

but some are strange and wonderful

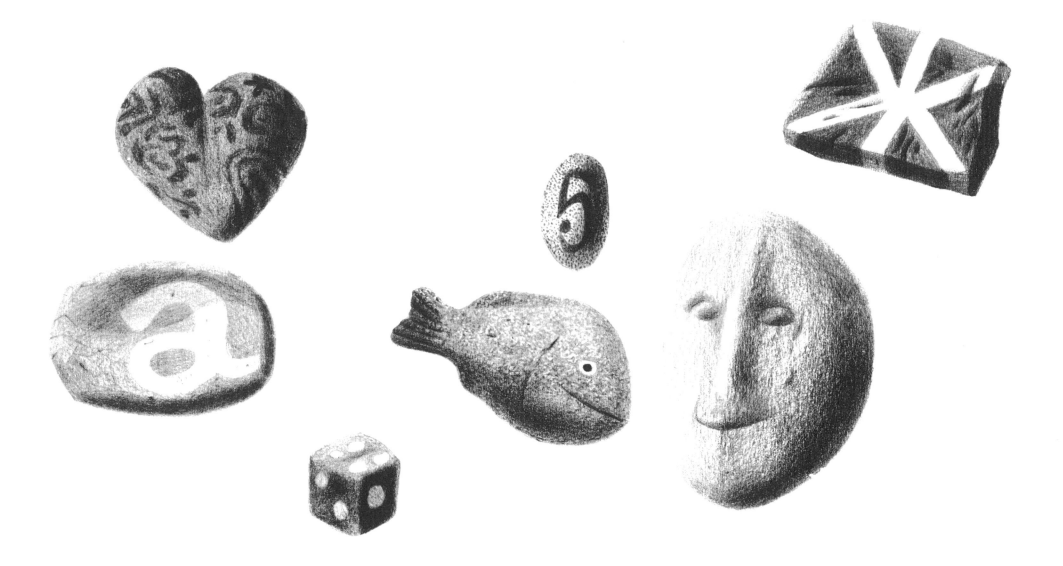

There are fishpebbles

and goosepebbles

numberpebbles

and peoplepebbles

and many letterpebbles

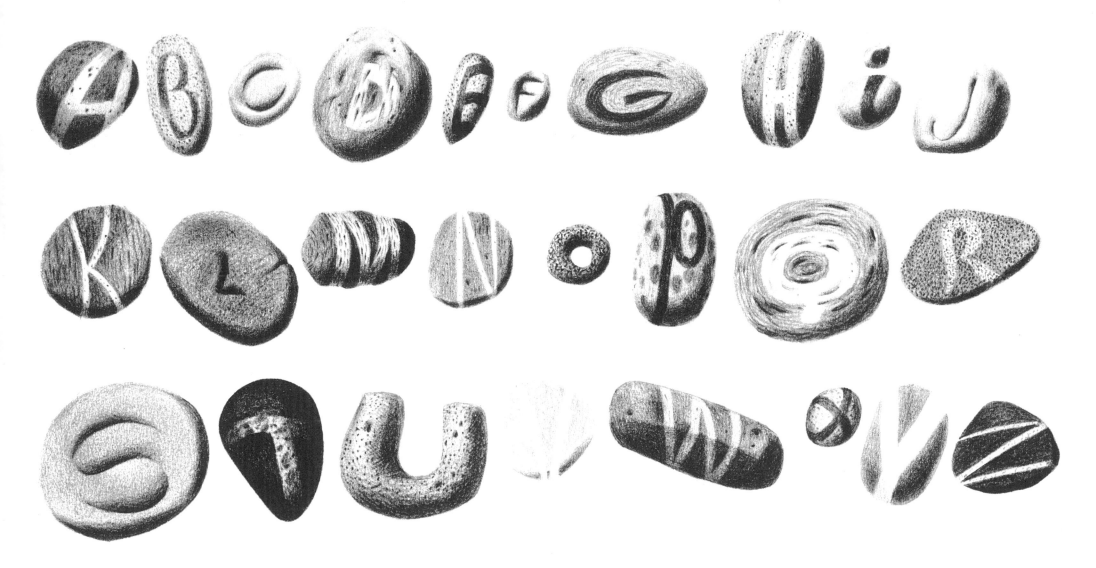

DEAR JOHNNY
HOW ARE YOU I AM WELL
I GATHER PEBBLES
ON THE BEACH · SOME
LOOK LIKE LETTERS
BUT I ALSO FOUND
A AND A M

a seal

and a clock

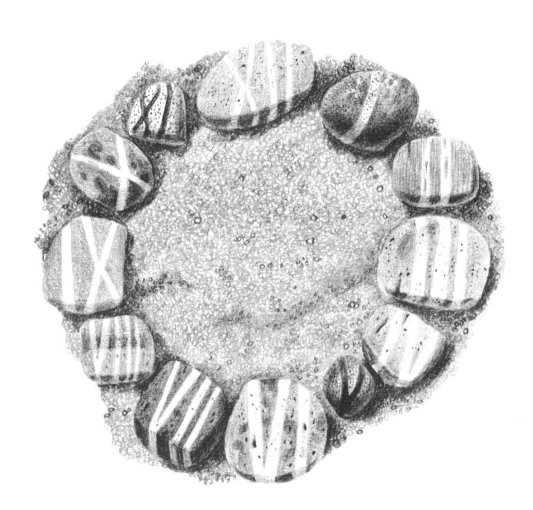

Why don't you go out on my beach and look for other pebbles?

More Picture Books
by Leo Lionni
from Mulberry

Inch by Inch. A winsome, winning inchworm, proud of his ability to measure anything under the sun, must think fast to escape a hungry nightingale. (ISBN 0-688-13283-9; $4.95)

Little Blue and Little Yellow. Here is a fanciful story that captures the joy and pleasure of friendship between two children as it introduces certain basic concepts about color. (ISBN 0-688-13285-5; $4.95)